Tomie dePaola

Strega Nona's
HARVEST

G. P. PUTNAM'S SONS
PENGUIN YOUNG READERS GROUP

For Greg and all the fine folks
at Spring Ledge Farm

G. P. PUTNAM'S SONS
A division of Penguin Young Readers Group.
Published by The Penguin Group.
Penguin Group (USA) Inc., 375 Hudson Street, New York, NY 10014, U.S.A.
Penguin Group (Canada), 90 Eglinton Avenue East, Suite 700, Toronto, Ontario M4P 2Y3, Canada
(a division of Pearson Penguin Canada Inc.).
Penguin Books Ltd, 80 Strand, London WC2R 0RL, England.
Penguin Ireland, 25 St. Stephen's Green, Dublin 2, Ireland (a division of Penguin Books Ltd.).
Penguin Group (Australia), 250 Camberwell Road, Camberwell, Victoria 3124, Australia
(a division of Pearson Australia Group Pty Ltd).
Penguin Books India Pvt Ltd, 11 Community Centre, Panchsheel Park, New Delhi - 110 017, India.
Penguin Group (NZ), 67 Apollo Drive, Rosedale, North Shore 0632, New Zealand
(a division of Pearson New Zealand Ltd).
Penguin Books (South Africa) (Pty) Ltd, 24 Sturdee Avenue, Rosebank, Johannesburg 2196, South Africa.
Penguin Books Ltd, Registered Offices: 80 Strand, London WC2R 0RL, England.

Published simultaneously in Canada. Manufactured in China by South China Printing Co. Ltd.
Design by Marikka Tamura. Text set in Adobe Jenson.
The art for this book was created with transparent acrylics on Arches 140 lb. handmade watercolor paper.
Library of Congress Cataloging-in-Publication Data
De Paola, Tomie.
Strega Nona's harvest / Tomie dePaola. p. cm.
Summary: After helping Strega Nona plant her vegetable garden just so, Big Anthony takes some extra seeds
and sows another garden willy-nilly, then must find a way to deal with the consequences.
1. Strega Nona (Fictitious character)—Fiction. [1. Vegetable gardening—Fiction. 2. Gardening—Fiction.
3. Witches—Fiction. 4. Magic—Fiction.] I. Title.
PZ7.D439Ssm 2009 [E]—dc22 2008046366 ISBN 978-0-399-25291-4
Special Markets ISBN 978-0-399-25581-6 Not for resale
1 3 5 7 9 10 8 6 4 2

It was spring, and all the snow had melted. The rich earth was beginning to warm. Strega Nona pulled out a small wooden box that had been hidden away in the dark cupboard all winter.

"Aha," she said as she took out small packets of seeds she had saved from last year's garden. "*Qui siete, i miei amici piccoli*—here you are, my little friends."

"Why were all those seeds in the dark, Strega Nona?" Big Anthony asked.

"Well, *mio caro*—my dear," Strega Nona answered, "they had to rest, just like you do, so they will be able to do their job when we plant them in the garden."

"When will we plant them, Strega Nona?" Bambolona asked.

"When *la luna*—the moon—tells us, Bambolona. Then we will plant each kind of seed carefully in the right place. After all, we can't just throw the seeds into the ground in a big pile! A garden must be orderly so it is easy to pick the vegetables."

"Now, let me look in my *libro di giardino*—Garden Book—to see what we did last year."

Every year, Strega Nona wrote down in her book what she planted, when and where. She never put the same vegetables in the same spot.

"We have to move them around," she told her young helpers, "so the soil will stay happy and strong. But first, Anthony, you must spread the compost and manure we saved all winter and rake it into the soil so our vegetables will grow as big and beautiful as can be."

So, Big Anthony put a clothespin on his nose and did his job.

"Children, come," called Strega Nona. "It is almost the end of *Maggio*—May—and there will be a full moon tonight. It is time to plant. Now, Anthony, I want you to make nice straight rows in the soil with the end of the hoe. That's where the seeds will go."

"Big Anthony," Bambolona scolded, "you're not making the rows straight enough. You know that Strega Nona likes everything Perfect!" She added, "And so do I!"

Bambolona is so bossy, Big Anthony thought. *Someday, I'll show her I can do something perfect, too.*

That night, when the full moon rose in the sky, Strega Nona quietly crept out to the garden. She looked up at the moon and sang:

O *Bella Luna*, smile on me,

And on the seeds I sow,

And let the moonbeams shine from thee,

To make my garden grow.

"And now for the *ingrediente segreto*—secret ingredient."

Strega Nona blew three kisses to the moon.

"Oh," said Big Anthony as he watched her. Suddenly he spied some seeds that had dropped on the ground. "I know. I'll plant my OWN *perfect* garden behind the goat shed. I'll *show* Bambolona!"

So, Big Anthony poked some holes in the ground. He threw in the seeds and covered them with compost and manure. He watered and watered.

Then he sang Strega Nona's song:

        O *Bella Luna*, smile on me,

        And on the seeds I sow,

        And let the moonbeams shine from thee,

        To make my garden *really* grow.

He blew the three kisses to the moon. And just to be sure, he blew three more.

As it did every year, Strega Nona's garden grew beautifully.

Big Anthony's garden   *Strega Nona's garden*

Soon, bright green *insalata*—salad—was on the table.

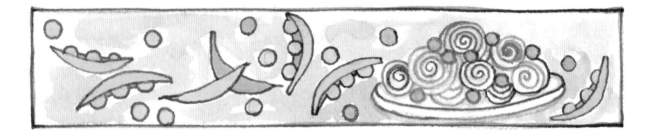

Fresh peas were added to the pasta from Strega Nona's pasta pot.

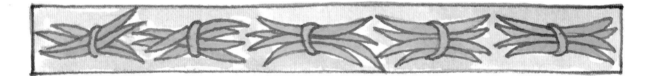

Green beans were cooked in olive oil.

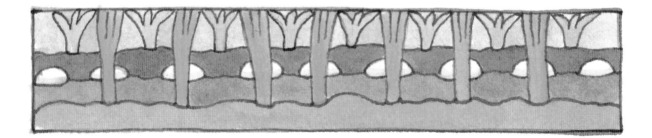

And the other vegetables were growing beautifully, too.

Big Anthony's secret garden was growing as well.
But not quite so beautifully. It looked like a jungle!

Mamma mia, Big Anthony thought. *I can't let
Bambolona—or Strega Nona—see this mess!*

Big Anthony's garden   *Strega Nona's garden*

Now it was time to harvest the vegetables that Strega Nona would keep over the winter.

It wasn't long before the root cellar and the rafters in the kitchen were full.

"*Molto bene*—very good!" said Strega Nona to Bambolona and Big Anthony. "A job well done. We all deserve a good rest."

But Big Anthony didn't have time to rest. He had other work to do.

"I've got to pick all my vegetables. What will I do with them?" he said.

The next morning, when Strega Nona opened her door,
she found a big pile of vegetables.

"*Santo cielo*—good heavens," Strega Nona said.
"Where did these come from?"

She called Big Anthony and Bambolona. "My children, please
carry all these vegetables into the kitchen. *Grazie*—thank you."

Every morning there were more vegetables outside the door.
Soon, there was hardly any room to move in the kitchen.

Maybe these are from the villagers, Strega Nona thought. *Perhaps they had too good of a harvest. Well, I must find out—and soon. If this goes on, I won't have room to sleep in my little bed at night!*

The next morning, Strega Nona packed a basket of vegetables. "I'll take these to the Sisters at the convent and maybe they'll know something."

"Oh, *grazie*, Strega Nona," the Mother Superior said. "You must have heard our prayers. Our garden didn't do well this season. In fact, no one's garden in the village did. We had too much rain down here, while you had lots of sun on your hill."

So Strega Nona went right to the mayor.

"Sì—yes, Strega Nona," Signor Mayor said. "The harvest was poor
this year."

"Well, I have more than enough to share," Strega Nona said. "I will have
a Harvest Feast tomorrow evening at sundown. Tell everyone to come."

And Strega Nona practically ran up to her little house.

"Bambolona, Big Anthony, come quickly," Strega Nona said. "We have much work to do. I am going to have a Harvest Feast for all our friends and neighbors. We shall share our bounty!"

"Evviva, evviva—hurrah, hurrah for Strega Nona!" everyone shouted.

"Arrivederci, buonanotte—good-bye, good night,"
Strega Nona and her two helpers called out.

Strega Nona looked around at her empty kitchen. "Well, that took care of that," she said with a smile. "But I still wonder where all those vegetables came from." And she climbed into bed.

Later that night . . .